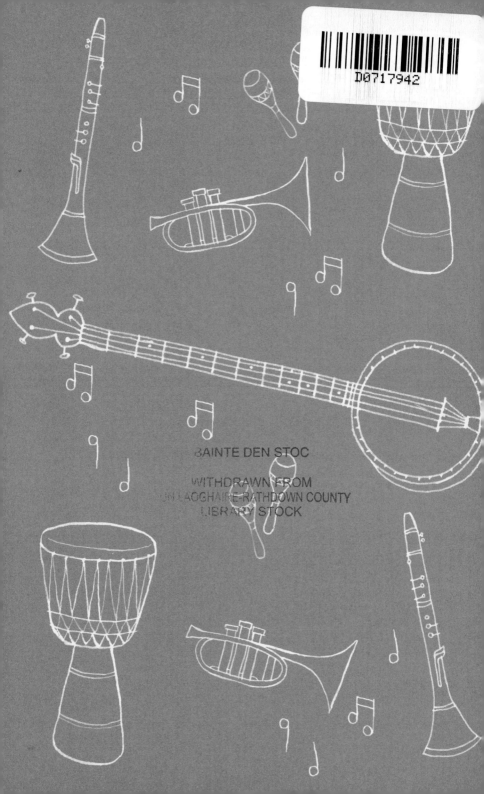

A Rather Remarkable Grizzly Bear

Marco
Moonwalker

Praise for the *Marco* books:

'very touching and well written tales
about a boy and his friend'
The Irish Times

'a compelling story'
Sunday Independent

'a madcap narrative'
Sunday Business Post

'a beautifully told, engaging tale, about Ireland's
favourite, lovable grizzly bear'
Armadillo Magazine

'an all-round brilliant book...'
Albert, age 11, for *Books Ireland*

 **Gerry Boland** was born in Dublin but has lived in north Roscommon since 2001. He teaches creative writing in national schools in the area, works part-time in a local organic community garden, and spends as much time writing as he can. He is a commited environmentalist and an active campaigner on vegetarian and animal rights issues. His first collection of poems, *Watching Clouds*, was published by Doghouse Books in June 2011, and he is working on a collection of short stories. He is also the author of two travel books on Dublin.

Marco

Moonwalker

Gerry Boland

Illustrated by Áine McGuinness

THE O'BRIEN PRESS
DUBLIN

First published 2012 by The O'Brien Press Ltd,
12 Terenure Road East, Rathgar, Dublin 6, Ireland.
Tel: +353 1 4923333; Fax: +353 1 4922777
E-mail: books@obrien.ie
Website: www.obrien.ie

ISBN: 978-1-84717-301-0

1 2 3 4 5 6 7 8 9
12 13 14 15 16

Layout and design: The O'Brien Press Ltd
Cover illustrations: Áine McGuinness

Printed in the Czech Republic by Finidr Ltd
The paper in this book is produced using pulp from
managed forests.

The O'Brien Press receives assistance from

Dedication

to Miriam

Acknowledgements

Thanks are due to the following: to everyone at The O'Brien Press for their expertise and dedication and their belief in the Marco stories; to Áine McGuinness for her brilliant and funny illustrations; to the Tyrone Guthrie Centre in Annaghmakerrig; to my sister, Mary, and my brothers, John and Joe, all three of whom have been unfailing in their support and encouragement; as always, to Miriam.

Marco
Moonwalker

I was in the house one morning when I heard the sound of Mum's trombone coming from the garage. I went outside and sat on the back step and listened. She was playing a tune I hadn't heard before. It was hard to describe – kind of sad and lonely, but beautiful too. The sort of tune that gets into your head and stays there.

She didn't stop playing, even when I turned the door handle, which was loose and made a lot of noise. I opened the door a little, stuck my head through the gap, and couldn't believe what I saw.

Marco was sitting in the far corner, playing Mum's trombone. He had his eyes shut and a sort of faraway look on his face. It was the same expression that he wore whenever he was thinking about his old home in the Rockies.

I closed the door and tiptoed out again.

A little while later Marco came in to the kitchen to make himself a cup of tea.

'Marco.'

'Patrick.'

'What was that tune you were playing on Mum's trombone?'

He nearly dropped the teapot he was holding.

'Don't tell your mum I was playing her trombone. She'd be mad.'

Mum never got mad, at me or at Marco. Especially at Marco. She thought Marco could do no wrong.

'I didn't know you could play the trombone. Did they teach you how to play it in the zoo?'

'They didn't teach me anything in that place. There was a tune in my head … the trombone was on the shelf … so I played it.'

'You played a tune that was in your head on a trombone that you never learned to play? Marco, you're a genius.'

'I am?'

'A true genius. That probably means you can play any instrument.'

'I don't think so. The music that was in my head was a trombone sound.'

'Don't you hear any other instruments in your head?'

'I had a tune in my head yesterday that wasn't a trombone sound.'

'What was it?'

'A banjo, I think.'

'Are you sure it was a banjo?'

He closed his eyes for a long moment. I could tell he was playing the tune in his head.

'Definitely a banjo,' he said.

'Jamie's dad has a banjo,' I said. 'He lives just down the road. I'll ask if I can borrow it.'

Ten minutes later we were both back in the garage and I had a banjo in my hand.

'Here, have a go.'

He took the banjo from me. It was tiny in his big paws.

'I'd rather you didn't watch,' he said. 'It makes me nervous if you're watching.'

I went and sat on the concrete step and gazed across the garden. Moments later I heard some strumming. Soft strumming, then hard strumming. He was trying out the different sounds. The strumming changed to plucking. The chords changed, too. I was listening to a grizzly bear learning how to play the banjo, all by himself, with no music book, no teacher, without ever having held a banjo in his life.

Half an hour passed. I watched the sun go in and out of the clouds that were rushing across the sky, as if they were late for work. With every minute, Marco was getting better and better. I could just make out a tune.

'Is that the tune that's inside your head?' I called back in to the garage, without turning around.

'That's the one. I'll need a good bit of practice.
The banjo is trickier than the trombone.'

All through the day I could hear him practising.
He was still at it when I went to bed at ten.

By teatime the following day, anyone calling to the house would have thought that the world's greatest living banjo player was playing for free in our garage.

Listening to him play, an idea came to me. It was a crazy idea, but those were the ones that I liked best. I wasn't very good at lots of things – apart from making a nice cup of tea – but I was the world's best at coming up with crazy ideas.

We'd have to disguise him, of course. The duffel-coat with the enormous hood that he wore the night he escaped from the zoo was just about big enough to cover his body, but it wouldn't be long enough for what I had in mind.

Mum would have to make super-size black pants with wide legs that went right down to the ground, covering his big hairy feet.

If we went ahead with my crazy idea, we'd be out a lot, and there'd be loads of people looking at us, especially at our huge, amazing-looking trombone/banjo player. We'd have to have a name. It came to me straightaway: The 3Ms – for Marco, Mum and Me. I liked the sound of 'The 3Ms'. Short and catchy.

All this was going through my head as I lay in bed that night listening to Marco playing the banjo and the trombone in the garage. It was still going through my head when I came home from school the next day. Marco had stopped playing by then and was back in his usual place, on the sofa in front of the TV. He was watching a Michael Jackson DVD.

'Michael Jackson,' he said, as I sat down beside him.

'What about him?'

'He was strange.'

'Strange but brilliant.'

'I love the way he danced. I've been trying it out. Watch.'

He paused the TV, then stood up and did his own version of the Moonwalk – the Grizzly Bear Moonwalk – across the living room carpet. It was hilarious, easily the funniest thing I'd ever seen. He made me laugh so hard I thought I was going to burst. I really did. I couldn't breathe. I couldn't even speak to tell him to stop.

'What's so funny?' he said, stopping at last.

It took me a minute to get my breath back.

'If Michael Jackson saw that, he'd probably die a second time. That was priceless, Marco.'

He sat back down and we watched the rest of the Michael Jackson DVD. He concentrated really hard, trying to see exactly how Michael did the moves.

'One day I'll be able to dance like that,' he said.

I decided that now was as good a time as any to break the news.

'I'm forming a band. You. Mum. Me. We'll be known as The 3Ms.'

Marco had a funny way of smiling. Unless you knew him, you wouldn't be able to tell if he was smiling or if he was angry. His mouth didn't move, but the fur around it did, just a teeny bit, enough that you'd notice. His nose twitched a few times, and his eyes got a little brighter.

'And what will *you* be doing in this band of
ours?' he said.

'I don't know yet. I might learn to play the guitar. And percussion, definitely percussion: the drums, timbales, maracas, spoons and forks.'

'Spoons and forks? I thought you used spoons and forks to eat.'

'You can bang them together and make a cool sound, too.'

'If you ask me, it doesn't sound like a great band.'

'Mum will be the lead singer, and she'll also play the trombone. You can play the other instruments.'

'What other instruments?'

'I was thinking of the electric violin, the piano-synthesizer, and maybe the saxophone. If you can learn the trombone and the banjo in a day, you'll be able to play those, no problem. Maybe the double bass too.'

'It's a crazy idea, Patrick. How can a bear play in a band? I'd be spotted straightaway. And then the zoo would bring me back.'

'You won't be spotted. You'll be unrecognisable. I have it all worked out.'

'What does your mum think?'

'She doesn't know yet.'

'Aw, Patrick!'

'What? Mum will love the idea of us forming a band. And she'll get us all the gigs. She knows everyone there is to know.'

'I don't know, Patrick. It's all too sudden.'

'But aren't you getting bored of being in here all the time, watching TV? Think of it, Marco. You could be a **star**!'

And the funny thing is, he was a star. The moment he blew on that trombone or sax, or plucked the banjo, or played the electric violin, the crowd went wild. They whooped and yelled and then they went really quiet so they could listen to his solos. They liked Mum, too, they clapped their hands and whooped and yelled every now and then, but they never went wild. They only went wild over Marco.

As for me, well, I didn't mind not getting whoops and yells. I was having too much fun being part of The 3Ms and watching the crowds go wild over Marco.

We were playing the Town Hall one Saturday night. It was a full house. As usual, everyone stared at Marco. We had him well disguised. He wore the loose black pants and a really cool purple cape over his hooded duffel coat. Mum had made this sort of super-hero black mask with eye-holes so that Marco could see out, but nobody could see his bear face.

No one could have guessed that behind the disguise was the missing grizzly bear from the city zoo. He looked fantastic, standing there on stage, all eight feet of him, playing the trombone, the sax, the electric violin, the banjo, the piano-synthesizer.

Backstage, after the gig, there was a loud knock on our dressing-room door, and four of the largest men I had ever seen barged in, almost knocking me down.

Behind them marched Sergeant Calloway and Constable Strummer, the two policemen who had come looking for the missing grizzly bear when Marco first came to our house. And right behind them came our next-door neighbours, Sadie Sharp and Nosey Blunt.

It turned out that Nosey and Sadie had seen
Marco a couple of nights earlier walk across our
back garden and go into the shed.

He was wearing his 3Ms costume. Mum had told them that the famous musician who was gigging with us was staying with us for a while, and they were hoping to get a look at him without his mask. The last thing they expected to see was the mega star musician re-emerge as the missing grizzly bear from the zoo.

Of course they rang the police. And that was the end of The 3Ms. It was also the end of Marco's freedom.

I waited a week before I visited him in the zoo. I was too upset, and I knew he'd be in a pretty bad state. To be back in the zoo was Marco's worst nightmare.

The 3Ms had been a great idea, and while we were on the road it was fantastic, but if we'd stayed at home Marco would still be living with us. Which is all he ever wanted. It was me who wanted more. I felt really guilty.

I took a bus to the zoo early on Saturday morning. It was drizzling and I was the first one in the queue at the entrance, waiting for the gates to open. I went straight to Marco's enclosure. He saw me coming and came over to the fence. There was no one around, not even a zookeeper.

'What a disaster,' he said.

'It could be worse.'

'How could it be worse, Patrick?'

I tried to think of something worse, to cheer him up, but I couldn't.

'I know things don't look great right now,' I said. 'But the good news is, I have a plan.'

'You and your plans, Patrick.'

That's all he said. He could have said that it was my plans that put him back in the zoo. But Marco would never do that. He was too nice.

I looked at his face. I had never seen him so miserable. 'Actually, this is Mum's plan, Marco. It's a good one. She's already started working on it. We should have you out in a fortnight.'

'What's a fortnight?'

Marco was super-intelligent, but there were some things he could never get right. Time was one of them. He had no idea what a week was, and if I told him I was going away for a month he'd probably expect me back in an hour.

'Soon. A fortnight is soon, Marco.'

His face brightened up a little. Marco thought Mum was great, and if she had a plan, maybe it would work.

There was no one nearby, so I took out the flask and the two plastic cups I'd brought with me. I poured Marco a cup of tea with milk and no sugar, just the way he liked it, and passed the cup through the bars of his enclosure.

'Who made the tea?' he asked.

'Mum.'

'No offence, Patrick, you make a nice cup of tea, but your Mum's is the best. Tell her thanks.'

He held the cup in his paws and drank slowly, enjoying every sip. I handed him a couple of chocolate biscuits and then I poured myself a cup of tea. The two of us were quiet for a few minutes, just drinking our tea and eating our biscuits.

By the time I left he was looking a lot happier.

Mum indeed had a plan. She had been in contact with the director of the zoo. He was excited about the idea of a life-size statue of Marco. She told him she would need to measure Marco. He said that she could come and go as she pleased, and that the keepers would give her all the help she needed.

41

A week later, she had two life-size moulds made, one to be delivered to the zoo straightaway, and the other that she would use to make the statue.

The zoo director agreed it would be good publicity to place the mould inside Marco's enclosure, so visitors would see it when they came to see Marco. Mum said she'd be taking it back the day she delivered the completed statue.

On the morning the statue was to be delivered, Marco opened the mould and removed the fibreglass replica of himself that Mum had made secretly and left inside.

It was the spitting image of Marco, right down to the colour of his fur. He placed it by the large boulder that he often stood beside. Then he went back to the mould, climbed inside, and closed it.

Half-an-hour later the zoo opened its gates for the day, and an hour after that, Mum's statue arrived in a delivery van.

A big crowd came to see the statue being delivered. The Prime Minister, who never missed a chance to get his picture in the papers and his face on the evening news, was there. There were dozens of TV cameras and lots of reporters from all different countries.

Marco's return to the zoo had been big news, especially after he'd been uncovered as the third and most famous member of The 3Ms.

Mum was there, of course, standing beside the zoo director. When the statue was unveiled, she was given a big round of applause.

In all the excitement, nobody took any notice of the four big strong college students that Mum had hired to take the mould away.

They carried it past the crowd, past the Prime Minister, past all the TV cameras and reporters, and out the gates.

Then they loaded it into the van and off it went.

Mum told me all this later. I had stayed at home, to be there when the van arrived, and to show the students where to put the mould.

By the time it was discovered that Marco was missing, me and Mum and Marco were deep in the forest that covered the Chocca Mountains, way up north.

We'd left our van in the upper car park and had hiked twelve miles up the mountains, into thicker and thicker forest. Marco carried the tent and ninety per cent of the food that was to keep us going for a month.

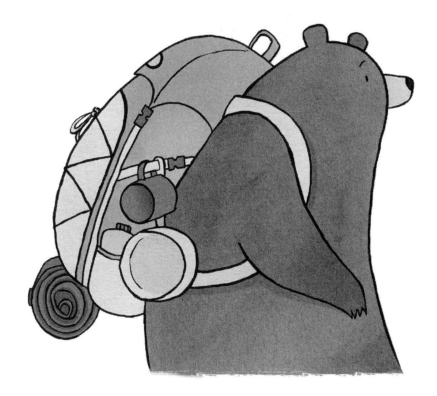

Mum reckoned that all the fuss would have died down by then and that it would probably be safe to go back home. That was the plan.

We found the perfect place to make camp and to pitch the tent. It was a lovely piece of soft grass beside the top of a short waterfall.

Marco spent most of his days at the bottom of the waterfall, catching fish. I spent most of my days hanging out with him. It was the best of times.

Mum had brought some books that she wanted to read: books about sculpture, about the legends of jazz, a few history books, and a book about Michael Jackson.

It was June, and the sun shone every day, and for one whole month we didn't see a single person.

Every night before we went to sleep, Mum read a chapter of the Michael Jackson book to the two of us, but mainly she read it for Marco.

Then, one beautiful, fine sunny day, Mum decided that it was time to go home.

I clambered down the rocks to Marco. He was lying in the sun, fast asleep. I didn't like to wake him, but I had no choice.

'Marco, wake up.'

He opened one eye and looked at me.

He knew straightaway. He was so clever.

We're going home.

'We're going home,' he said.

'We are,' I said.

'That's good. I miss the TV. I miss your mum's trombone playing. I miss my shed. I miss everything about the house.'

'Me, too,' I said.

Half-an-hour later, the three of us were packed and ready to go.

We didn't want anyone to spot us on our way down the mountain, so we waited until the sun went down.

Marco went first, as he could see really well in the dark.

We were sad to be leaving the Choccas. We knew that we wouldn't be coming back for a long time, maybe never. But we were happy, too. It felt good to be going home.

A week has passed and things are almost back to normal.

Marco is digging a tunnel from the shed all the way across the garden to the garage. Mum got a man in with a jackhammer to make a hole in the concrete floor of the garage where Marco's tunnel will emerge. Soon he'll be able to come and go as he pleases without having to worry about being seen by Nosey Blunt or Sadie Sharp.

The director of the zoo rang an hour ago and spoke to Mum. He told her that there were huge crowds coming to see the Marco statues every day. He thanked her for doing such a brilliant job.

'By the way,' he said, 'I've been meaning to ask you. Why did you make a second statue? No one here can figure out why you made two statues when we only asked for one?'

Mum always knew this question was going to come, and she was ready for it.

'I wasn't happy with the first statue,' she said. 'The fur wasn't quite right. So when the second one was perfect, I decided to let the zoo have it. I didn't have anywhere to put it, in any case.'

The zoo director obviously wasn't very smart because he didn't even think to ask how the second statue got into the enclosure. He swallowed Mum's story completely.

'It's a gift,' she said. 'Marco was such a fantastic character that the zoo needs two statues to make up for the fact that he's no longer there.'

I always knew Mum was clever, I just didn't know how clever. That makes two geniuses in the house!

So, Marco is safe here with us, and no one suspects us for getting him out of the zoo. I can't wait to tell him, but I don't want to interrupt him. He's in the living room right now, watching the Michael Jackson DVD, and practising the Moonwalk. He's very determined.

My guess is, by the end of the week, he'll be moonwalking all around the house.

If Michael Jackson were alive, he'd probably be jealous.